I0712690

Blood Ties

A Collection of Three Covenant of Blood Shorts
J.S. Living

Book design by Giulia Calligola

Editing by Leah Rambadt

Artwork by Dini Luna

Library of Congress Control Number: 2024921735

ISBN 979-8-9857001-2-1 (eBook)

ISBN 979-8-9857001-3-8 (Hardback)

www.thejsliving.com

Dedication

For the Black people who read and write historical and urban fiction, this one's for you.

Themes and Warnings

*B*lood Ties includes themes and discussions that may trigger individuals such as, but not limited to: Racism and slavery; offensive language; death; child abuse; attempted murder of a child; and contemplation of suicide.

About Blood Ties

I've always wished for more from my favorite books. I wanted more writing from my favorite authors; more in-depth information about my favorite characters; more artwork depicting my favorite characters; and more about the universes created in the books that I loved. More. More. MORE.

Now that I'm the author, I can provide these things to you, my readers. For all of you, my little Bloodlings, I offer MORE.

This short story collection provides answers to some questions you may have about The Covenant of Blood, also known as CoB. This short story collection provides answers to some questions you may have about The Covenant of Blood, also known as CoB.

Answers about what it's like for Liz when she's trapped as Lizzy's subconscious. An explanation about what happened to Dmitri on the day he asked for permission to marry Lizzy. And what Angelo's motivations for following through with the wedding were.

Why only three stories?

With more stories set in the Bloodlines universe to share, I don't think it would be right to piece them together in such a short time.

You're probably also trying to figure out why I set each of the stories in different years and, in Angelo's case, a completely different century.

It's simple: These are the short stories that called to me the most while I was writing *CoB*. I also thought sharing these thoughts would provide you with an understanding of these characters' motivations throughout *CoB*. Like, seriously, I wanted y'all to understand why Liz was so desperate to switch places with Lizzy. To understand the roles of Vlad Dracula—aka The Impaler or Vlad Dracul—and the witches' role in Dmitri's inability to tell Lizzy who he was. And to shed light on Angelo's silent acceptance of marrying a stranger, a union imposed by supernatural law.

Without these stories, we wouldn't have answers to those questions. And let's be real—y'all wanted to know too.

So, here are those answers. Please read and enjoy these three short stories about some of my favorite characters. This collection, the size of a novelette, is my gift for you, my beloved Bloodlings.

Of course, if you still have some unanswered questions, contact me via email at info@thejsliving.com OR through my contact form at www.thejsliving.com. I'm also on social media as @thejsliving. I hope to hear from you all.

Happy reading!

XOXO
J.S. Living

Contents

A Thought for Lizzy, My Alter Ego

There's something to be said about being cursed by witches. Because 'tis what this is: a curse. Witches gave my family the ability to turn into soul-sucking creatures who damn others to hell. And, for those of us with a more—how can I put it? Ah, yes. Volatile nature. The witches gave us the extra special ability to manifest as an additional consciousness. We have thoughts, feelings, and even a corporeal form within the mind, but we're not exactly people.

'Tis funny, Lizzy, I'm stuck in your subconscious mind while you get to live a full life. I only come out when your mind is too weak to handle what life has thrown at us.

I should be the one out there.

I should be the one learning to control our powers.

I should be the one attending practices with Andrei.

I should be the one falling in love.

But 'tis never me. Instead, I get to deal with the nasty stuff.

I get to make the big messes.

I get to tear people to shreds.

I get to be covered in blood.

I get to be unhinged.

But I don't always want that. Sometimes, I want to be the soft one. You may not know this, Lizzy, but I'm your protector. Stuck in the back of your mind until you contact me.

One day, we'll be two separate people. But, for now, I'm stuck in here and you get to live out there.

A Tuesday Training in 1593

Liz's Story

Our body thumps to the ground as Lizzy misses yet another easy shot. If I were in control of our shared body, this wouldn't have happened.

"This is easy," Andrei says for the millionth time.

And he's correct. What he's teaching her is simple. Lizzy just isn't practicing enough.

"If it was so easy, I think I would have figured it out already," Lizzy scoffs at him.

We scoff at him.

'Tis an interesting feeling, sharing a body. I can feel everything she feels. I can see everything she sees. Smell everything she smells. But 'tis not the same as living. Everything is like an echo. I know what's going on around me, but I don't have a say in what's being done.

"It is easy. You're just not trying hard enough." Andrei crosses his arms. "Try again." His voice is stern.

He means business.

The thought belongs to Lizzy. Funny how I can hear her thoughts, but she can't hear mine. Trying to talk to her is like screaming into a void—pointless and a waste of energy.

She blows a puff of air and moves our hair out of our face. I'm unsure why she bothers. Between the small gusts of wind and her struggle to control her powers, 'tis just going to be in her—our—face again.

Why is he always like this?

Because, I try to tell her, *you're not taking this seriously enough. This is our livelihood, and you need to get on board.*

But 'tis no use. She can't hear me.

"I am going to try again. Place him there." Lizzy uses our hands to gesture to the man in front of us.

Andrei follows her instructions and sits the man on the ground. He takes off the man's blindfold and raises an eyebrow.

"What are you?" The man asks, gasping for air as he takes in our surroundings. I don't have to be in control for me to read his thoughts. He's staring at the weights, ropes, and poles mingled with bows and arrows for archery, swords, and other weapons. He wonders what use a woman has for such things, questioning why they are in a courtyard typically reserved for sipping tea and eating small delicatessens.

"Do not worry about that," Lizzy says with our lips. "Now hush, please, sir. I must practice."

Andrei's eyes are on us as we walk toward the man. We crouch in front of him and stare directly into his dark eyes. We *must* compel this man if we want to eat. I know how, but since Lizzy and I can't communicate at the moment, she has to learn for herself.

When the witches cursed Mother's side of the family with the sluagh abilities, they didn't know entities like me would be born into the subconscious mind. They didn't know we would be strong. Nor did they know the truth of what we are capable of. To them, we were beautiful mistakes, meant to rot in hell with the same souls we condemned. Instead, we possess the power to suck the souls of the damned and convert their energy into powerful blasts.

But while I know the truth, dear little Lizzy is unaware of what we can do. She only knows of our vampiric nature from Father's side, and that we don't burn in the sun because we are part human. She knows not of the sluagh and fairy blood that courses through our veins from Mother's side—four bloodlines mixed to create a perfect creature.

We're capable of the same things, but I have more knowledge of our ancestry, of our past, than she does. There are still some things I have questions about too, though. 'Tis one reason I've been trying to convince her to find our Mother. Although, it most likely serves no purpose now. If our Mother wanted to be in our lives, she would have responded to our letters.

"What are you going to do to me?" A loud beating of his chest accompanies the man's question. He is clearly terrified.

Does he think I am going to hurt him? Lizzy again.

Of course he thinks that, I try to tell her. *We **are** monsters, after all.*

She doesn't hear me.

"I am just trying out a little trick," Lizzy tells him in the kindest voice we can muster. "You do not mind, do you?" She stares harder into his eyes and watches them glaze over.

I do the same. In my case, 'tis either look through our shared eyes or create illusions for myself. Being stuck on this side is like being in a big black box. I can create anything I want or do anything I want when I don't want to take part in my alter ego's activities. But, just like everything else, 'tis a deception. 'Tis not real.

"Now," Lizzy says through our shared mouth, "I am going to untie you, and you are going to forget that you were ever here. Got it?"

The man nods his head.

As if he has a choice.

"Wonderful," Lizzy says. "But before I do that, I am going to drink some of your blood."

This amuses me. I want to see how far she gets this time without my help.

"My blood?" The man's voice is soft and dreamlike.

"Yes," she says, "your blood." I feel our teeth extend. She reaches our hands out and exposes his neck. She locates the vein and moves toward it.

The smell of his blood is intoxicating. 'Tis so strong it permeates through the barriers that separate Lizzy and me. For a moment, I feel like I'm in control.

That happens sometimes. A scent, an idea, or an event will be so strong that, for just a moment, I become the dominant personality.

I wonder if this will be one of those times.

And this man is special. His blood is potent, yes, but so is his soul.

What is this stronger scent? Lizzy thinks.

'Tis his soul, I inform her. But I still don't have enough presence for her to notice me.

She lets go of his neck, trying to find the source of the smell, but 'tis difficult.

"What are you doing?" Andrei asks. He flares his nostrils, hardens his eyes, and crosses his arms.

Why is he angry?

"You're supposed to be learning how to compel and drink in a timely manner," he chides. "You're already over your time."

But Lizzy doesn't care, and neither do I. We are both trying to call that scent back to us. 'Tis a primal need to feed on his soul. I'm just excited she's finally cognizant enough to seek it out.

I've always had to wait until Lizzy was asleep to feed on souls. But now, now she'll be able to do it for the both of us.

"Shh," she commands Andrei. "There is something off with this one."

"Something off?" Andrei's nose twitches as he sniffs. "He smells fine to me."

"Not with his blood, you imbecile," Lizzy says with our mouth.

He must have struck a chord. 'Tis rare for her to use words like "imbecile" to describe Andrei.

"'Tis something else," Lizzy mutters.

The nature-like smell tinged with desperation and guilt is headier than the smell of man's blood. But before she can explore it further, a dark presence appears at the east side of the courtyard, shifting Lizzy's focus.

"Elizabeth Mina Bathory-Tepés, do as I say and finish your task."

The voice doesn't belong to Andrei. It belongs to the scourge of Wallachia, the great Vladimir Tepés, our father. Although, he's more Lizzy's father than mine.

When he first discovered my presence, he wanted nothing to do with me. He said I was an intrusion on his daughter's life. If he knew the number of times I've saved her ass, he wouldn't have spoken to me like that.

Wouldn't speak to me like that.

Why can't he treat me like his own? I may be a subconscious mind, but I have feelings, too.

"But—" Lizzy starts.

"No buts," Father says. "You can't expect to always live a human life. We Dhampir…"

"I know." Lizzy rolls our eyes.

We've heard the same story since our childhood: We're Dhampir and, as such, we can live without feeding on blood until our twenty-fifth birthday. But, after that, we must feed regularly. Hence, this little feeding lesson.

But our loving father knows our other secret. I've told him that, because of our sluagh origins, soon enough, souls will be just as important to consume. Maybe that's why Lizzy is getting this lesson now.

Lizzy moves closer to the man. The smell of his soul is hard for her to ignore—hard for me to ignore.

There! We scream the word together as a glittering white light moves into our vicinity. Or, rather, we feel it.

"A soul," she whispers.

She finally knows what it is.

Lizzy takes her hand and plunges it into the center of the man's chest.

"No!" Father and Andrei scream.

Yes, I scream, clapping my hands in elation.

They're too late to stop her, to stop *us*.

Lizzy grabs the soul, leaving a wide, gaping hole in the spot where the silvery light was. She caresses it with our hands and smells it.

This is it, she thinks. ***This** is what I was looking for. But what do I do with it?*

Eat it, I say.

Who said that? Lizzy's thoughts tinge with confusion.

Don't worry about the who, I reply, *just do as I say.* I grin, and I know Lizzy can feel the smile form on my face because she cringes a bit. *I don't bite,* I tell her. *At least, not much.*

Why do you want this? Lizzy holds out the soul, pondering what to do with it.

We want this. 'Tis sustenance.

Sustenance? Confusion again.

Yes, I say. Is she ever going to understand what we are, what we can do? *We are sluagh*, I continue. *We eat souls.*

Since when? Curiosity this time.

Since forever. But I don't have time to explain it to you. The soul. 'Tis losing its luster.

But I don't understand.

Of course she doesn't. Lizzy's cursed too and doesn't even know it. *Ask Andrei,* I tell her, urging this conversation to move along. *I want to taste the soul.*

But what's your name?

You never remember I exist. I say this because 'tis true—this isn't the first time our minds have crossed paths.

I will.

Fine. 'Tis Liz. Now... But I trail off because she's gone. The connection cut off. I look through our eyes to see what's happened.

Andrei and Father whisper to each other. They're talking about souls. About us. About *me.*

Their faces are red and puffy with anger, and I laugh. That's what they get for not telling Lizzy about me sooner.

Take a bite. Take a bite. Take a bite. I repeat it over and over, hoping my influence gets through. And it does because Lizzy caresses the soul once more before taking a huge bite out of it.

Thank the universe.

The taste of the soul explodes in our mouth. Every part of our body tingles, and we let out a moan of gratitude. I close my eyes and absorb the soul into my being. This man has done bad things, but not enough of them for me to condemn his soul to hell—another job foisted on me by those damn witches. No, I'll have to wait until he achieves what his heart desires most before that can happen. Instead, I add his soul to the collection as a reminder to find him upon his deathbed and consume the rest. The partial soul we ate can't convert into energy until I've devoured every piece. After all, soul collecting is a long, arduous process.

We look at the man, who has passed out again. It must be the trauma inflicted upon him by entering my collection.

But then he sits up, his eyes fluttering open again.

"Where am I?"

The wind blows and something feels different. I sniff the air. This isn't an echo of pine trees. I'm actually smelling them. I smile and stretch my hands, happy for this moment of freedom from my dark prison.

"Don't worry," I say with a grin on my face. "You're safe."

A Poem to My Love

A woman of death—
A queen of the world, the woman I love.
She is the dearest of dears,
The sweetest of sweets,
The bloodiest of blood.

She outshines the moon and the stars,
Outruns the fastest of creatures,
Will outlast me and this dreadful world.

I, however, am but a man—
Born into poverty, raised to greatness,
Destroyed by those closest to me.
Brought up in fire and brimstone
And turned into ash.

I come from nothing.
Will be nothing.
Am nothing.

Nothing but her provider of blood,
Her lover of the flesh.
Her best friend born of sacrifice—

Her confidant of rituals past,
The only person who understands her suffering.
I am the servant who survived the bloodshed.

I am Dmitri Kovács

A Death Day in 1600

Dmitri's Story

I can't believe I'm meeting Elizabeth's father in an official capacity for the second time in my life—or that this meeting is happening today. I'm madly in love with her, but we can't get married until I meet him: the master of this estate, the man who haunts the dreams of children, The Impaler. Or, more accurately, Lord Vladimir Tepés. The Impaler was the moniker given to him after an unfortunate run-in with the Boyars during the Easter Feast in 1457 when he impaled them and their wives. It was well before my time, but people talk—so much so, it is a joke among servants to call him The Impaler when he makes unreasonable requests. I will not make that mistake tonight—even if a part of me is nervous that I'll somehow botch this whole thing.

Breathe, I remind myself. *Look at this lavish bedroom you're in. You, sir, are in the Ottoman Empire, one of the greatest nations. And you know **the** Vlad Dracul. You are going to do great.*

The self-supercilious talk works.

I pull my long hair into a knot. I'm still lost in how I got to this point. Who would have thought a former slave who started with nothing could work his way up the ladder and become a free man ready to propose to Vladimir Tepés's daughter?

All it took to meet the love of my life and to gain this room in Vladimir Tepés's castle was making my way as a slave from Africa to Hungary, learning multiple languages, and threatening a powerful vampire. It was challenging, but it was worth it to meet Elizabeth.

My Lizzy.

The most beautiful creature in the world. And I don't mean "creature" endearingly. I mean, she's *literally* a creature of the night. A wonderful mix of vampire and sluagh, but with the warmth and caring of humans.

She is rich, powerful, charming, gorgeous, and completely out of my league. In my native language, she would be called "belo monstro"—a beautiful monster.

I use my fingers to brush the edges of my hair back and consider donning the turban I purchased. But turbans are *only* for Ottomans, and I am not one. My confidence from earlier dissipates. For a moment, I forget I am nothing. I come from slaves, and my station in life was determined worthless before I was even a babe. Yes, this room within Vlad Dracul's castle is nice, but it is not *my* castle. I do not own it.

I am not like the others in this fortress, the ones who come from well-bred Ottoman families. No. I was just lucky enough to be purchased by Lord Tepés at the young age of seven.

I grimace, remembering those first ten years of servitude and learning everything I could about the stronghold and the man who imprisoned me. Like I said, I was planning to kill him. I figured in a worst-case scenario, someone would kill me for staking a self-important, aristocratic, elitist vampire. Death seemed better than vassalage.

I pull on the loose, dark green trousers I purchased from the merchant and smile. Who knew Lord Tepés would call me a survivor and give me a chance others like me only dreamed of after that incident? It was a chance to win my freedom.

And that was when I met her.

"This is my daughter Elizabeth," Lord Tepés had said. "Survive her for seven days, and you can have your freedom."

"Survive her?" I asked.

"You'll see what I mean."

And I did. Lizzy was a brat, especially at night when it seemed like some other being had possessed her. On those nights, she'd insist on feeding even though she didn't have to, and I had to abet her. It was awful. I frequently asked myself, why was I taking orders from someone three years younger than me?

I put on my golden trouser socks and shine my grey riding boots. When I'm satisfied with their luster, I put them on too. I check the lighting outside. 'Tis almost time.

Time is a funny thing. I thought I'd die from all the near-death experiences Lizzy put me through. But I didn't. I survived. And, after seven days, I won my freedom.

And winning my freedom was everything.

It meant I could choose where I wanted to work. I could choose what I wanted to do with my life. For the first time, I had prospects. I could leave the castle, build my home, find a job, maybe create a family.

But the world wasn't ready for that yet. No, 'twas safer to stay at the castle and learn everything I could about the affairs of the world. It took years of poring over maps and books and paintings—about six years, I'd say—but I learned to read and write. I learned how to cook, how to hunt, how to fend for myself. And on my twenty-third birthday, I became Lizzy's blood bag.

I know it sounds abhorrent, but it paid well, and I was the only one who could handle the then twenty-year-old.

Please do not misunderstand. She didn't *have* to feed; but it was the beginning of the five-year lessons of teaching her to control her powers.

I tuck in my linen undershirt and don a golden inner kaftan. "Damn," I say aloud, "how many buttons does this thing have?" I shake my head and begin buttoning the garment.

Lizzy's dresses aren't even this difficult to button. I should know.

On one of those days when I would go to her room to let her feed on me, we became something more.

I'm not sure when it happened. Maybe it was when we sat playing a children's game from my homeland. Maybe it was when she showed me the secret to building wealth in an empire that would see me dead. Or maybe it was the day we kissed for the first time.

Somewhere in all that, our relationship bloomed. We became friends. And, eventually, lovers.

I check my clothing again and tie my royal blue silk sash around my waist. Initially, I thought the colors would be garish on me considering the hue of my skin, but they aren't. I can almost pass for royalty, or at least a rich lord. My neck feels tight, so I tug at the collar of the inner kaftan. I'm not used to clothing with buttons, especially a garment with this high neck. The merchant promised it would make me look regal, so I took him at his word. He failed to mention it would feel like I was choking. For clothing that costs as much as two homes and several animals, I hope it is worth it.

As someone who comes from nothing, I feel confident that the amount of lei and piaştri I spent on this could have gone to a better cause. Then, I remind myself that even if my clothing is expensive, 'tis what I do with my position of power that's important. And after tonight, I will solidify that position with my charm and my wits.

I grab my outer kaftan from the top of the chair in my small room in the castle. The filigree print on it reminds me of summers back home, which is why I purchased it as well. 'Tis long and heavy, but I have a feeling tonight will be cold.

"Okay," I tell myself while adjusting the sleeves of the blue and gold outer kaftan. "I can do this."

I step out of the small space, turn around, and give the room one more look. 'Tis eerie.

This place was my home for so long. But after thirteen years of slavery, fifteen years of being free—six of which I spent learning about the world and how to take care of myself and nine of which I used to work and save coins—I am confident enough to leave this home.

The business venture I've started will be enough to support Lizzy and me for as long as we live. Today will be the start of our new life. All we need is her father's blessing.

"Right then." I close the door and make my way to the Grand Hall. Someone set the room up just as I thought it would be. Bright candles, glittering dinnerware, and other accoutrements make for a magnificent display. All of this is for my Lizzy's birthday.

I wipe my sweaty palms on the kaftan, wondering if my beloved Lizzy will recognize me in this attire.

"Dmitri," Lizzy calls to me as she walks into the room.

I gawk at her. Her dark skin, an oddity in these parts for someone of Ottoman blood, is glistening. I'm not sure how, but she has adorned her face with gems. They form a butterfly around her eyes. And her dress. Was it imported? It must have been. The top half is like a corset and the bottom is voluminous, much like the dresses I see the royalty from the Western empire wear from time to time. The dress is white at the top and descends into greys and blacks toward the bottom. 'Tis unique.

She embraces me and kisses me on the cheek.

"Elizabeth," I say. I pull away from her, just for the moment, and take her hands.

She smiles at me. "Are you not going to say something?"

"Words escape me, my love."

She laughs. "As they should."

I grin at her and push back a strand of her silky, dark hair. The texture reminds me of the women who nursed me to health when I was young. "I'm always amazed at how much you look like me," I tell her. I don't mean for it to slip out. 'Tis rude to say something like that to the one you wish to marry, but sometimes I can't help myself. I have an innate need to speak my honest feelings to her.

But instead of frowning, Lizzy laughs. "Yes," she says, "there have always been questions about my parentage. Questions that have yet to be answered. But did you know that all of us—Ottomans included—are descendants of your people?"

I frown. No Ottoman would ever claim to be a part of *my* lineage. And even if they were, they do not know our struggle. I smile tightly, remembering Lizzy is not of the human world, and sometimes she's unaware that what she says can be insensitive. "Even if that were true," I respond in the kindest voice I can muster, "no Ottoman would agree."

"I would," she says.

She must read the seriousness of my tone because she follows up with an even more shocking statement.

"I know you think me naïve, Dmitri, but I have seen it."

"You have seen what?" She piques my curiosity.

"A woman of pure Ottoman blood bore a child with skin as dark as yours and mine. When asked about it, she swore she did not know why the child came out like that."

The thought of what she's describing concerns me. "So, what happened?"

"They investigated whether she had been faithful. A warlock—one who posed as a priest," she elaborated for my benefit, "came to confirm that she'd remained faithful to her husband. He concluded she was, in fact, being honest."

"So, where is the babe?"

"Unfortunately, they sent the child off to be raised by the slaves. They swore everyone in the room to secrecy."

I ponder her words for a moment. "If they swore everyone to secrecy," I muse, "how is it you came across this information?"

She smiles wickedly. "The warlock and Father were having a conversation. I overheard it. Apparently, this was not the first time."

"This has happened before?"

Lizzy nods. "Sometimes it occurs." She fidgets with her dress. "It has even happened with some slaves. They bear children with skin as white as porcelain."

"And where do those children go?"

"Wealthy families adopt some of them. The wives, who are usually barren, say they are going on a trip with their husbands—or they make up some other excuse, and nine months later reappear with a babe. They tell their friends it was a miracle, but really, it is a cover-up."

"Sounds like a conspiracy."

She shrugs. "Perhaps. But it happens."

"And the ones these wealthy families don't adopt? What happens to them?"

"Convents or churches in other countries take them in. They're in suitable homes."

"So, they receive the opposite of the first child you told me about..."

She frowns.

"Sorry. This is your night and I'm ruining it."

Lizzy's frown deepens. "Never apologize for pointing out unfairness in the world," she says. She kisses me on the cheek. "Without you, I would be ignorant of the ways of the world. Father keeps me sequestered away. I am surprised he allows you to be so close to me."

"It is only because my job was to feed you," I point out.

"True, but I am appreciative."

"As am I," I reply, glad the serious aspect of our conversation is over.

"Anyway," she says in a slightly more cheerful voice, "I assure you that, despite my parentage, my looks are genuine. Save for the rouge lipstick applied by my maids and the jewels on my face."

"Maybe we can find those answers together," I tell her.

"Perhaps so." Lizzy looks around, and then points. "There. I have found Father. Shall we go outside to speak to him?"

"Yes," I say, wiping my palms once more on my kaftan. "Let's go."

"Right." She grabs my hand and leads me outside. As we approach her father, Lizzy asks, "Are you sure you are ready?"

"I am," I nod. And 'tis the truth. I am ready to speak to the man I hope will be my father-in-law.

"Father," she calls to Lord Tepés.

"Elizabeth," he replies, walking toward her, "how are you enjoying your party?"

"It is truly magnificent, Father."

"Wonderful. You know I would do anything for you."

"I know, Father," she gives him a hug. "Which is why I want to introduce you to someone. Dmitri?"

That's my name. I clear my throat and approach. "Yes, Lizzy." I try to slow my heart down. We practiced this. It should go smoothly.

"Father," she turns back to Lord Tepés, "I would like you to meet Dmitri Kovács."

"Dmitri..." Lord Tepés's voice trails off. "Why does your name sound familiar?"

"Well, sir," I say, taking a deep breath, "I tried to murder you once." I didn't practice this line, and it is definitely not a good way to begin this conversation.

Elizabeth looks at me in alarm before turning back to her father. "What he means is—"

"Ha, ha," Lord Tepés laughs. "I remember you. Such spunk you had as a child."

"Yes, sir," I say, releasing a breath I didn't realize I'd been holding.

"And you've done well for yourself since then," he continues. "You won your freedom, and now I hear you have amassed a small fortune."

"Yes, sir, all of that is true." My body loosens up. I didn't know my muscles could strain this tightly, but clearly, I was more tense than I needed to be.

"So, Elizabeth, what's this about? Did you come to sing his praises?"

Lizzy shifts in her dress. "In a way, yes," she says. "Is that all right?"

"It is." Lord Tepés turns to me. "Whatever you need," he says, "name it and I shall provide it."

"Thank you, sir," I say. This is it. This is the moment. "There is... Well, there is one thing."

"Well, spit it out."

"I would ask for Lizzy's hand in marriage. You see—"

"No."

"No?" I repeat like an idiot.

"No. Elizabeth shall marry no one. Least of all you."

Lizzy's smile turns into a frown. "But Father," she says.

"I said *no*, Elizabeth," Lord Tepés said, his voice as boisterous as thunder.

"But, Lord Tepés," my voice trails off as I struggle to find the right words.

"Excuse me," he says, stalking off.

Lizzy follows him, and the two of them argue. I walk over to join the conversation, hoping I can change his mind.

That's when I hear it.

'Tis an odd sound that occurs whenever the other one comes out. The dark half of Elizabeth. The half that calls herself Liz.

I know little about Liz—only that she comes out to feed every so often, and she takes over whenever Lizzy becomes overly passionate about something. This must be an overly passionate moment because I hear rumbling, the telltale sound of a storm brewing.

"You can't do this," Liz says.

"I can, and I will," Lord Tepés replies.

"You won't!"

"It is for the best."

"What would you know about what's best for me?" She crosses her arms defiantly.

"I know better than you think. Did you really believe I would let you marry him?"

I try to find a moment to interject, to plead our case, but all too soon, I am being escorted by the castle guards.

"Hey!" I yell at them and attempt to get out of their grip, but they are far older and far more powerful than me. "What is this?"

"You'll find out soon enough, Dmitri," Lord Tepés says, unconcerned.

As I'm hauled toward the castle, Liz lets out a scream I've only heard once before.

It is bloodcurdling.

The last time I heard her scream like that, everyone within her radius had bloodied noses and ringing ears.

I shrug the guards off me while they're distracted by holding their ears. "We have to get out of here!" I yell at them. They don't know what's about to happen, but I have an idea.

They try to grab at me, but they're thrown off balance by a second scream piercing the air. The outside of the castle rumbles.

That's two.

I run.

If she screams one more time, we'll all be dead. I find my way to the one place in the castle that is safe—the tunnels.

The third scream splits the air. The pungent odor of sulfur and smoke permeates the area as everything crashes around me.

Suddenly, I'm lying crushed under the rubble. I'm able to remove some of the stone trapping me. But when I finally reach my leg, 'tis disfigured. The rubble has twisted and mangled it into an unrecognizable lump of flesh. I try to move it and gasp as pain shoots up through it. I can't leave in this condition, and I don't have the required materials to fix it. The realization sinks in.

I'm stuck.

Hours go by. Maybe even days. 'Tis hard to tell when you're stuck underground in the dark, losing blood.

But, eventually, someone finds me.

"This is your fault," a male voice says.

I recognize it. "Lord Tepés..." I try to say. My voice is dry and raspy.

"Hush boy," he says. "Drink this." He holds up a cannister of liquid.

I drink it gratefully. "Why are *you* the one down here?"

"Because you're the only survivor," he says, taking it back.

My mind races with a thousand questions, but the word "survivor" stands out. "Elizabeth!" I yell. "Lizzy!" Of course, there is no reply. "How is she?" I ask, looking around to see if I can spot her. "Is she safe?"

"She's fine," Lord Tepés says.

"But you said..."

"Apologies. I meant you're the only *human* survivor."

I gulp and close my eyes, waiting for the crushing weight on my chest to subside. Panic does not look good on me. "That's good," I say. "That's good." With the knowledge Lizzy is safe, I can ask my next question. "Lord Tepés," I say.

"What?"

"Earlier, when I asked about you being down here, I was…I wanted to know…what I meant was: Why are you, personally, down here? You've never cared about my life before. And I can't imagine—"

"My daughter already hates me," he says, cutting me off with no preamble. "She would hate me more if I left you to die."

"Aren't you…soulless," I ask in the most respectful way I can.

He takes a deep breath. "Yes. But there are, as you say, remnants of emotions. Like an echo. It fades a bit every day."

I stare at him in shock. This is the most I think he's ever spoken to anyone outside his inner circle. "If that's the case—"

"Sleep, boy," Lord Tepés says. "Sleep."

And, as if compelled, I do.

When I wake up next, there are witches surrounding me. I rub my head, which aches. Then, I look down at my leg. "'Tis healed," I say.

"Yes," a woman says. "It took a while, but I healed you."

I take in my surroundings, a dark stone room with skulls decorating the walls. 'Tis small, and filled with herbs, tonics, and bones. We must be in the healing room under the catacombs, about three miles from the entrance to the tunnels. "And you are?" I ask, worried by the fact I'm essentially in a grave.

"Mira," she says. "And you're Dmitri."

"I am." I try to sit up, but she pushes me back down.

"You won't heal properly if you try to move now."

"Why are you healing me in the first place?"

"Because I'm a witch. We heal people." Mira unwraps the bandage around my leg.

"But Lord Tepés dislikes me." My mind is fuzzy, but I distinctly remember him forbidding me to marry Lizzy. Which… "Where is Lizzy?" I ask her.

"If you mean Elizabeth," Mira says, frowning, "She is not of your concern." She cleans the wound and re-wraps it.

"Of course she is. I am to wed her."

"The Impaler will not allow it," she says blankly.

"And yet I plan to proceed."

Mira sighs. "And what will you do when you are of old age and Elizabeth looks the same?"

I consider her words. It never occurred to me that Lizzy will be forever young. "It doesn't matter," I say. "I will love her until my last breath."

"You would have her mourn your death?"

"Marriage is in sickness or health. In life and death. We've already discussed it, and Lizzy has agreed."

This seems to amuse Mira, but she says nothing.

"What's so funny?"

"Nothing," she says. "I'm just happy to hear your answer, is all." She finishes up with my leg and walks toward the head of the bed. "It is admirable." She kisses me on the forehead and says, "He's ready for you."

"Dmitri." Lord Tepés, who appears seemingly out of nowhere, says my name like 'tis a curse.

"Lord Tepés," I respond curtly. Perhaps the rumors are true. Perhaps he *can* materialize out of thin air.

"How are you feeling?" He eyes me carefully.

"I feel well enough to fight for Lizzy's hand in marriage."

Lord Tepés sighs, and for the first time, I see his true age. But I don't let that discourage me.

"Will you sanction it?"

"I cannot," he says.

"You can," I sneer. "'Tis what Lizzy wants. You promised her anything."

"NOT THIS!"

"Then why save me?" I yell, trying to stop my voice from shaking. "Why do all this?" I gesture at Mira, my leg, and the cot I lie on.

"Mira," Lord Tepés gestures to the witch.

Mira smiles. "Elizabeth has an interesting future ahead of her," she says.

"And am I a part of that future?" I shouldn't ask, but I must know.

"'Tis...unclear."

"How is it unclear?" I tilt my head at her.

"Decisions are key," is all she says.

"What decisions?" I raise a brow at her.

"That is for you to figure out," Mira says. "I am simply here at the request of Lord Tepés."

I turn to him. "What am I missing?"

Lord Tepés massages his temple. "I'm going to regret this. But, after Elizabeth's...display...I can't ignore it anymore. I must request a favor of you."

"That wasn't Lizzy," I mutter.

"I know," he replies. "It was Liz. Which is why this favor is important."

"What is it?" What kind of favor would someone like Lord Tepés need me to do?

"Yes. A favor from you."

It takes a moment for me to understand his words. "And if I complete this favor, I can marry Lizzy?"

"With the coven's permission...yes."

I look between Mira and Lord Tepés. "What do you mean?"

"Your new business venture," Lord Tepés begins, "you plan to locate missing people."

"Yes," I say. "I am skilled at it."

Lord Tepés rubs his hands together and paces around the room. "Yes, I have heard of your success." He pauses.

I wait for him to continue. When he doesn't, I raise a brow at him.

"Right," he says, "I need you to find Elizabeth's mother."

"You want me to...why?"

Lord Tepés frowns. "Liz is becoming more volatile. I don't know how long I'll be able to help Elizabeth contain that menace. But there are other reasons too."

"What reasons?"

Lord Tepés is a careful man, and Elizabeth Bathory is his soft spot. From what I gather, they haven't spoken in years, so if he's asking me to do this, it must be important. And if 'tis important, the more information I have, the better.

Besides, I don't want to go into business with someone who plans to renege on a deal.

"None that I can speak of right now. Can you find her?"

"Yes. But I don't know how long it will take."

"As I expected." Lord Tepés strokes his chin and turns to Mira. "Let's do it."

"As you wish, Vlad Dracul, the Impaler of Wallachia."

Lord Tepés glares at the witch, but she ignores it.

"What are we doing?" I avoid making eye contact with the two of them and ignore the weight in my chest and the ache in the back of my throat. I wish time would speed up so the feeling of dread in the pit of my stomach will go away, but it doesn't.

Mira grins. "Two things. First, I'm going to give you the type of abilities humans only dream of."

"You're going to turn me into a monster."

She shakes her head. "Not at all. You'll still be human. I am simply giving you the tools you need to go up against creatures of the night—or supernaturals, as they will be called one day."

I nod. "And the second thing?"

"Immortality," she says.

My mouth twitches, but I try not to grin at this news as my chest lightens, a welcome reprieve from the tightness I experienced earlier. I smooth my clothes, hoping to contain my surprise and excitement at the prospect of being able to stay as young as my future bride. "I won't be able to die?"

"Maybe immortality is the wrong word." Mira rolls over a table covered with herbs and other objects and sits on my bed. "You'll still be able to die," she continues. "It will just be difficult to kill you, nearly impossible, actually. And," she mixes ingredients in a bowl, "you'll be able to live for a long time. How long, well, that will be up to you."

I look between the two of them again. "And what is the catch?"

"You must find Elizabeth Bathory and make the young Elizabeth fall in love with you for a second time."

"Make Lizzy fall in love with me a second time?"

"Yes. Someone notified her of your death and, therefore, won't know who you are. Not until you gain her trust, break her heart again, and still convince her to come back to you."

I take a deep breath and hold back the scream in my throat. Instead, I calmly respond, "Why are there so many stipulations?"

Mira isn't the one to answer me. Lord Tepés is. "Because this is my child. My daughter. I can't make it easy for you."

"You couldn't—" I laugh hysterically. "You couldn't make it easy? Love should be easy."

"Except it is not."

"Maybe that's why they call you The Impaler," I say. "Not because of the men you killed, but because you impale all those around you with your callousness and neglect."

"Do you accept the conditions or not?" Lord Tepés asks.

I grit my teeth. I have waited so long to call Elizabeth, Lizzy, my bride. What's longer?

"I accept," I say. "How do I know when I've completed the requirements of this pact?"

"I will be the judge of that," Mira says.

"What if you're dead?"

"Sweet Dmitri," she says, "I will never die."

"You don't know that."

"I know many things," she says. "Including what's in store for you and I."

"What are you talking about?"

"Shh," Mira whispers. "Let's save it for another time. Now, be a darling and hold out your hand."

I move my body as much as I can and hold out my hand. She cuts into my palm with a knife and drips my blood into a bowl. Then, she mixes it along with other herbs and pours the mixture over me while chanting a phrase from a long-forgotten language repeatedly. "Come, Vlad the Impaler," she says.

Lord Tepés frowns, but he obeys her anyway.

"Hold out your palm," she says.

He does as she requests.

She takes his hand and mine and presses them together. "Speak your names," she instructs.

We speak to them.

"May they be bound to their promise," Mira says, chanting another phrase. As she chants, my hand begins to sting and burn. The pain becomes more intense, but I grit my teeth and bear it. Even as the feeling of burning alive seems to consume me.

Before I know it, we've pulled our hands apart.

Mira wraps them with cloth. "It is done," she says.

"What now?" I ask.

"You're healed," she says. "And free to do whatever you like."

I take stock of my body. She's right. I feel more than better. More than a hundred percent. I feel like I can take on anyone. Even Vlad Dracul, The Impaler.

"Is this real?" I whisper.

"It is," Mira says.

"Ahem," Lord Tepés clears his throat.

I stand up and stretch my body out before assessing him. I feel like I could take him. Except this isn't the time. I made a promise. "Yes, Sir Vladimir Dracula," I say, using his older name.

He does not seem to expect this because his eyes narrow. "This is where the mother of my child was last seen." He removes some papers from his cloak and holds them out to me. "You can start here."

I take the papers. "I know the city well."

"Then get going."

"As you wish, master," I say.

I thank Mira and take the herbs she hands me. "Will I see you again?" I ask her.

"You will."

"I look forward to it."

"Me too." Mira smiles knowingly and presses her lips against my cheek. "I can't wait for this adventure," she whispers.

I pull away from her, suddenly afraid I've done something I shouldn't have. "Right then," I say. "I guess I better get to work."

I walk toward the door of the tiny healing room.

"And Dmitri," Mira says.

"Yes?"

"Change your name to The PI."

"Why…" But I don't have time to question it. When a witch gives you instructions, you follow them. "Will do," I say.

The PI. 'Tis a strange name, but I like the sound of it. The PI. The PI. Yes. When Lizzy and I next meet, I'll be The PI, and I'll make her fall in love with me again. I didn't mean to break her heart by almost dying, but I will do it on purpose if it means we get to be together. I just wonder how long I'll have to wait.

Remembering My Past

I hate living with a man who constantly experiments on me to make himself unbeatable and unkillable. But if he hadn't, I wouldn't be here now. Sometimes I wonder if that's a good thing or not. Let me explain.

I was barely even a month in the womb when he injected my mother with a so-called "medicine" that would stop her aches and pains—it didn't.

I was a year old when he tried killing me the first time—he failed.

And, when I was five, we went to the lake. I thought it was going to be a fun day in the water—it wasn't.

After all, he tried to drown me.

I remember being pushed underwater. I thought we were playing a game. But then, Father's icy hands held me under. I tapped his hand to tell him to let me up, but he didn't. I thrashed and kicked, to no avail. He would not let me up. Water rushed into my lungs. I couldn't breathe. The liquid invaded my lungs, and with every gulp, my consciousness faded faster and faster until I passed out.

I don't know how long I was out for. When I finally came to, I asked, "Why?" It was the only word I could muster.

"Because you are strong," Father said. "And because you cannot die. You, my son, will help me with my plan. Starting today, I shall train you as a soldier."

"What does that mean?" Itwas a naïve question. Even at that age, I knew what he meant. But I wanted to hear him say it.

"I will shatter, beat, and break you again and again until nothing phases you. Now, come my boy, we have much work to do."

It wasn't Father's words that frightened me that day, but the look on his face. The malice it held, the rage? Something bigger than himself possessed him. The other thing that terrified me was the plan he mentioned. After all, what type of plan involved the possibility of me, the son of the so-called "great" Ferenc Ndasdy, being killed?

I didn't know it then, but it would be hundreds of years before I got my answer.

Besides, I learned one thing that day: Always wear a smile on your face. That way, no one—whether friend or foe—will see the knife you're about to plunge into their back.

Placating A Parent in 2015

Angelo's Story

"**W**hat do you mean, the plan has changed?" I ask Anton while brushing my teeth with my electric toothbrush. I call him Anton because he's never been a true father to me, and he hates the name Ferenc. He used to tell me Ferenc was his past, before the betrayal and deceit; but Anton was his future as the greatest being in the supernatural world. I called him on his bullshit then. Let's just say he didn't take it well, so I never brought it up again.

Anton glares at my reflection from the doorway, the hallway stretching out behind him. Well, it's not a glare so much as the facial expression he gives everyone—the one that says not to question him. "Just what I said." He crosses his arms. "I am no longer sending you to kill Vlad Dracula."

I spit into the sink. "That's wonderful," I say. "I didn't want to kill one of the oldest vampires in history, anyway." Not that I have room to talk. I'm pushing somewhere in the mid-400s myself, but I'm not a vampire. I start a second round of brushing. There's only one way to keep up the appearance of being thirty, and that's good hygiene.

"I'm glad you agree," Anton says. "Because there's a more important task for you to do now that I've learned certain *information.*"

From my peripheral, I see him pacing up and down the hallway, muttering like a madman.

I spit into the sink again and rinse off my toothbrush. "And what's that?" I set the toothbrush on the sink, reach for the floss, and turn toward him.

He stops pacing and grins at me with devilish charms. "You're going to marry his daughter and impregnate her."

I drop the floss and stare at him. "Sorry," I say, slowly. "I'm going to be doing what, exactly?"

"You heard me," Anton says, his mouth spreading into an even bigger smile, this time showing all his teeth.

I hate it when they protrude like that. It's like he's mocking me. Or provoking me. Trying to manipulate me. Perhaps even all the above.

I don't like it.

And the way his eyes gleam with mischief...it's disturbing. Also, I just realized he's wearing his true face instead of the fake one Ida helps him hide behind.

"What am I missing?" I ask.

"I made a deal with the young Elizabeth," Anton says, clasping his hands together. "Told her I'd ask her for a favor if I helped her find her mother. After all, that's why she came here—to Atlanta, Georgia."

"And what do I have to do with that?" I can feel the floss I was using hanging out of my mouth, so I grab it and toss it in the trash. Anton's words are too important for me to ignore.

"After keeping her on edge for about seven months, I finally told her the favor was to marry you and bear your child."

"But why would she agree to that? We've never even met."

"No," he says, "you haven't. But..."

"But what?" He always does this. Leaves things unsaid so the rest of us will continue asking questions. I just want him to get to the point. "Tell me," I insist. My tone must be threatening because he narrows his eyes at me.

"Who are you to raise your voice to me, boy?" He stands up tall, stretching to his full height of six feet.

The lights in the hallway flicker in response. But whether it's because of his powers or because they need to be changed, I'm unsure.

"I'm sorry," I say. "I just wanted you to get to the point."

Anton gestures for me to follow him into one of the back offices of the church we live in. Yes, that's correct—a church. It's under construction indefinitely because Anton uses it to house us, his associates, and his thralls. The establishment itself is already large, but there's also an underground network of tunnels that leads throughout the city of Atlanta.

"Angelo, my child," he says in a lighter tone as he straightens some papers on the desk, "her blood runs through your veins."

His words echo in my mind, but I'm not comprehending them. "What do you mean by 'her blood runs through my veins?'"

"Your predisposition to...living," he spits the word out as though living is something I shouldn't be doing, "after someone kills you is thanks to her. Elizabeth Bathory-Tepés." He sits down in the office chair and spins toward me.

I stare at him, wide-eyed, and my jaw drops when I realize what he's saying. "The medicine that made Mother ill." I collapse into one of the overstuffed chairs in the room. "That was because..."

"Yes." He waves his hand dismissively and leans in toward me. "Because I injected her with the young Elizabeth's blood while you were still in the womb. Your mother, weak as she was, could still carry you to term." He laughs. "And could even care for you until your fourth birthday." He frowns. "Then she died on me like the worthless, mulatto whore she was. She left me with you." He scoffs. "The only one to survive my experiments. The only one who could carry out my plans to kill Vlad Dracula. Do you know what the best part is?"

I cringe in disgust, averting my eyes toward the beige carpet, but if I don't ask the question he wants to hear, this conversation might turn violent. I turn, direct my eyes toward him, and ask through gritted teeth, "What? What is the best part?"

"You're the spitting image of me, sans your darker skin tone. So, when you marry Elizabeth, the spitting image of Vlad Dracula's lost love, it won't just cause him mental pain, but physical pain as well. His heart won't be able to take it."

"A heart attack won't kill Vlad Dracula."

"No," he says. "It won't."

I cross my arms. "Then what's the point?"

"A heart attack will not be enough to take down the Great Impaler. However, being killed by his grandchild would."

This statement confuses me. "The grandchild you want me to have with his daughter?"

Anton nods. "A death befitting someone like him. Think about it, son. You'll no longer have to sacrifice yourself for my dream."

"But you'll sacrifice my future child for it?"

"Your future child will be Vlad Dracula's grandchild. He will never kill something so innocent."

The way he says "something," as though this future child is a plaything and not a being with thoughts and feelings, makes my skin crawl.

"I don't think I can do it," I say. I promised myself if I ever had a child, I wouldn't put them through the things Anton put me through. It wasn't great with Mother around, but it only got worse once she died. "I won't do it," I repeat, voice low with conviction.

Anton clasps his hands together and speaks in an equally low, guttural tone. "A little birdy told me you've been searching for a way to end your life." He paces the room, then stops to pick what I assume is dirt from under his nail. "It's such a waste to throw away a gift coveted by so many." He wipes his hands on his jeans. "But," he walks up close to me, "I'll tell you this." His eyes burn into mine, so bright they almost blind me, and snarls. "If you don't do this, I will destroy every piece of research you've ever collected. And," he pushes me into the office chair, pulling my long, curly hair so tight I have no choice but to meet his gaze, "I'll find the thing you love most, and crush it." He stomps his foot for emphasis. It's so hard, the entire floor shakes. "You *will* give me a grandchild," he says again, pulling my hair tighter. "Or I will make your life a hell on Earth. Understood?"

"Y-yes, Anton," I say.

He lets go, straightens his shirt, and leaves the room.

And that is how I ended up here a few days later, staking out my bride-to-be, Elizabeth Mina Bathory-Tepés.

Anton dragged me here—against my will, by the way—to the Coronation Ceremony for the Queen of the Realms. The readings of supernatural texts take two hours—just like at my coronation. Afterwards, the supernatural beings in attendance prick their fingers with a knife and let their blood pour into a bowl magically linked to Elizabeth's crown. And, also like mine, the more blood they give her, the more powerful she will become.

I was aware Elizabeth was to be my wife, but I was not told she was to be my queen as well. I try to hold back my laughter.

There is no way his plan will work.

I stand to the side of the processional line, watching people greet Elizabeth, our—*my*—new queen. I take a deep breath and brace myself to gaze upon the woman I'm supposed to be marrying.

I expect her to resemble her father, despite what Anton said. After all, if he waited this long to tell me about the blood pact he made, then surely the woman was going to be a miniature version of Vlad Dracula. Besides, there was no way Anton would find me a suitable marriage partner in terms of appearance.

Or so I thought.

She sits on a throne with a plush, red cushion with purple trimmings, greeting each being with a curt nod and returning their graciousness with her own.

The first thing I notice about Elizabeth Bathory-Tepés is how beautiful she is. Her copper, dark brown skin shines under the moonlight. Next, I see her thick, curly white-grey hair. It hangs past her shoulders and it's braided like the fairy folk. And with those pointed ears, she must have some type of fae in her family—a fairy or something else.

If all that isn't enough, the golden dust on her body glitters, and the etchings of runes around her wrists and ankles show she is powerful beyond measure, even without the offerings of the surrounding individuals.

It's cliché, but my heart literally stops at the sight of her. *Get a grip*, I tell myself. *Something has to be wrong with her for her to accept a deal with Anton.*

I stare at Elizabeth's clothes next, trying to see if they can provide any clue to what her personality might be like.

The black shift she's wearing is see-through. At first, this alarms me. From what I remember of coronations, the Queen of the Realms is only naked under her shift for the actual ritual, not for the after-party.

But upon closer inspection, I see she isn't naked. It's just the deep, blood-red coloring of the crop top she's wearing blends into her skin, making her seem naked in the dark. The crop top, or bralette as my last girlfriend would call it, accentuates the heart-shaped figure of her breasts.

Under the crop top, something glints.

It's a belly button ring. I hold back a smile.

That's new.

So, Queen Elizabeth likes body piercings. I file it away in my mind for later.

My eyes travel down to her waist. It's small, tiny enough I'm almost certain if I picked her up, my hands could close around it. Her hips balloon out, completing her hourglass figure.

Her tight black jeans have rips at the knees. I stare at them, wondering what it would be like to slip my hands inside the torn jeans and glide my hands up to the middle of her—I stop myself from going down that line of thinking.

This is an arranged marriage. Elizabeth is involved because Anton helped her find her mother. I'm only involved because I don't want my research to be destroyed. Sex for the sake of pure enjoyment is probably out of the question. At best, it'll probably be perfunctory.

After I've calmed my mind down, I glance at her shoes. But, somehow, she even makes red and black combat boots seem alluring. They accentuate her calf muscles, making me want to pick her up right now and take her as my own.

But this is the twenty-first century. It's not like it was when we were younger. Plus, she's a Queen now. I can't just demand her time.

"Again," I mutter to myself, "it's an arranged marriage. She will not fall for you."

"Give it time," Anton says, standing right next to me. "Soon she'll be begging you to do all the things you're thinking about right now."

I try to pretend like he didn't startle me, but it's no use. Anton always knows when he's gotten under my skin. "Nobody asked you," I mutter.

"Cheer up," he says. "I did this for you."

"You did this for yourself. And now you're threatening me." I cross my arms. "You're not cut out for fatherhood."

Anton frowns. "Angelo, my son, don't say that." He clasps his hands on my shoulder. "You are my world. Unlike your brothers."

I shove his hands off me. "I'll be dead before that statement becomes true."

He shrugs. "Perhaps. Are you ready to meet her?"

"Do I have a choice?"

"There's always a choice."

"One that doesn't end in my findings being destroyed?"

"Who can say?"

It's obvious what the phrase means, and I'm not one to play with fire. "Let's go," I say, walking to the back of the line to pay my respects to our new Queen of the Realms.

"We don't have to—"

"We're waiting our turn." It's petty, but if this is the only thing I can control about this day, I'm going to take it.

"Fine." Anton moves to stand in front of me. "But I'll be making the introductions."

"Whatever."

We stand in line for what feels like an eternity. But soon, someone passes the knife to us.

"Hello, Queen of the Realms," Anton says as we reach the front of the line. He picks the knife up, examines it, and sets it back down.

Elizabeth regards me with what I assume is disdain. Her scowl tells me she's already decided on me.

Unless she's checking me out...

My athletic build and towering height mean women usually throw themselves at me. Or, it could be my complexion throwing her off. People usually can't tell my ethnicity. When light hits me at a specific angle, I appear white; and when it doesn't, it's assumed I'm mixed race. But they never guess my lineage includes Italian, African, and Hungarian.

I look at her again.

It's scorn. She's staring at me with pure contempt.

"Oh, how rude of me," Anton gloats.

Gods, I hate when he gloats.

"This is Angelo," he continues. "Your *betrothed.*" He says it as though neither of us know we're engaged.

Elizabeth stares at him for a moment and then smirks. "I have achieved the power I need to break this pact," she tells him.

But Anton is still smiling, like he knows something the rest of us don't. "Even if that were true," he begins, "you have not done it. Which means something is holding you back."

I want to interject, but they seem to ignore me completely. I keep my thoughts to myself.

"No," she says, "I simply have not had the time since I have been pleasing my subjects."

Anton looks around and scoffs. "You mean our subjects."

"Excuse me?" Elizabeth glares at Anton, almost like she wants to squash him where he stands.

I hold back a laugh. What I wouldn't give to see that look again.

"I am sorry," she says, "I thought you said *our* subjects."

"I did," Anton says. "Or," he laughs, "this is rich. You don't know, do you?"

"What do I not know?" Elizabeth says through gritted teeth.

Whatever Anton is about to say is going to make her angry. I can feel it in my bones.

"Your mother and aunt didn't tell you?" Anton continues to belittle her, his laughter becoming guffaws. Eventually, he calms down and says, "The Queen of the Realms and the King of the Realms work closely together."

"Your point," she demands.

Anton paces in front of her throne.

I wait to see what he's going to say. Watching the two of them talk is like watching a ping-pong match—eventually one of them will lose the ball.

"The ceremonies are held at the same time for this reason," Anton continues.

"You are boring me," Elizabeth says, trying to affect a bored tone.

"The King of the Realms was announced today as well."

"Fuck," I mutter to myself, but neither of them hears me. He's about to tell her the news.

"Are you telling me *you* are the King of the Realms?" She sucks in a breath and waits for him to answer.

"Me? Hell no," Anton says, dismissive. "I would never participate in something like that."

He's telling the truth. Anton doesn't *have* to participate in these types of ceremonies. They just handed him the crown. But he refused it, too obsessed with bringing down Vlad Dracula to worry about caring for the supernatural community.

"But my son here is." Anton pushes me toward Elizabeth.

I almost stumble, but I catch myself and glare at my so-called father. Since I stand almost two heads taller than Elizabeth, she has to tilt her chin up to meet my gaze.

She regards me the way I'd regard a rotten apple—she wrinkles her nose and looks away.

"Don't look so disappointed," Anton says. "Angelo is nothing like me."

That is one thing we can agree on. I would never torture my kids the way he tortured me growing up. Being put on a rack and feeling your body stretch like dough until it breaks is not a fun way to spend a summer vacation.

"He will make a wonderful King of the Realms. And," Anton walks closer toward her throne, "an excellent husband."

Elizabeth fumes.

But Anton doesn't notice. Instead, he picks up the knife, stabs his hand, and drops an excessive amount of blood into the bowl.

He uses his own handkerchief to wipe the extra blood off his hands and puts it in his pocket. "I offer my blood to the Queen of the Realms, since she's going to need it." He hands the knife to me, and I take it.

Not wanting to cause further trouble, I cut my hand and let my blood drip into the bowl. For a moment, I think it swirls and turns golden, but it happens too fast for me to be sure.

Must be my imagination, I think to myself as I wipe the blood off on my handkerchief. Like Anton, I pocket the cloth instead of putting it in the discard pile. With supernatural creatures, you never know who to trust with your blood. I learned that at an early age.

Anton gestures for me to hurry, and I walk off with him.

"May the Queen reign for as long as she lives," Anton calls back.

I stare at Elizabeth one more time, pleading with her to realize I'm a pawn in this game, just like her.

But she turns away from me.

This is the woman Anton wants me to marry.

The woman he wants me to have a child with.

A child that might bring destruction upon the supernatural world.

If I do as Anton says, I will be free to look for a cure for my affliction. I'll be able to die. But if I don't, he'll destroy everything.

I consider this for a moment as we walk away from the festivities and toward the car.

The right thing to do would be to tell my father no. But he would just find someone else to do the deed. He'd alter the pact. I can't let that happen.

And Elizabeth seems to want to destroy my father just as much as I do. Maybe, just maybe, if I give into his wishes, she and I can both have what we want.

She'd get her freedom, and I'd get to continue looking for ways to die.

"Well," Anton says as we get in the backseat of our SUV, "did you make your decision?"

I don't answer right away.

"I'm waiting," he says, stretching his legs out.

For a moment, I consider my options. Then I bite my lip and clench my hands into fists before looking him in the eye. "I'll do it," I say. "I'll make Elizabeth Mina Bathory-Tepés my bride."

"That's my boy!" Anton grins happily and clasps my shoulder. "Get ready for a new dawn, my boy. When your son is born, everyone shall know the Ndasdy name."

I lay back in my seat and nod in agreement, but I'm only placating him. He is right about one thing though: Everyone will know the Ndasdy name. But not because we are great. They will know of us because of how we will die.

About the Author

J.S. Living has an MFA in Writing from the Savannah College of Art and Design. She enjoys binge-watching television, spending time with her cat, and, of course, writing like her life depends on it. Scan the QR code below for a special treat. Don't forget to follow the blood trail by subscribing to J.S. Living's email list and social media.

Twitter: thejsliving | IG & Threads: @thejsliving | FB: TheJSLiving | Website: www.thejsliving.com | Email: Info@thejsliving.com

Crowdfunding Supporters

I want to thank the following individuals for helping me crowdfund the hardback version of *Blood Ties: A Collection of Three Covenant of Blood Shorts*. Without them, this beautiful, fully edited, full-color version of the book wouldn't be possible. Thanks to your contributions, I'll be able to continue making significant stories. As always, I hope you all remain happy, healthy, and wealthy. Much love, J.S. Living:

Amanda; Amanda Balter; Anna McCluskey; Anonymous 1; Anonymous 2; Anonymous 3; Arledge Comics; Belinda Crawford; Catastrophi; Dead Fish Books; Iris Juylyenne; JC Spark; Jennifer L. Pierce; Kelsey; Kitkat Tenchi; Laura VanArendonk Baugh; Lafia; Lil Cam; Liz Sem; Nichole Barnum; Niels st; Sarah B.; Seven Dane Asmund; Shiloh W.; Stephanie Leader; Stephen Ballentine; Terri Schwomeyer; The Creative Fund by Backerkit; Valerie Lockhart, Esq.; William C. Tracy; Zelda Knight

Note: Those marked "Anonymous" were contributors who did not want their names posted on the crowdfunding page.

Acknowledgements

In addition to the crowdfunders, I would like to thank God, my family, and my friends for their unwavering support of my dreams. Mom, thank you for encouraging me to attend events and get my name out. Dashé, thank you for bringing this project to fruition with your donation and emotional support. Dewand, Jane, and Lakita—thank you for sharing the project with friends and colleagues. Aaron and Athena, thank you for being here for my journey in spirit. Another huge thanks to Raekwon and Soul for sending the project link through Discord and via text. I'm unsure how many people from your gaming and anime communities visited the page, but I appreciate the shout-out. I would also like to thank my former editor Michelle Rascon for putting me in touch with my current editor, Leah Rambadt. Leah did an amazing job churning out the edits for this project and was patient with my many delays. But, all that work paid off because here we are! Thanks so much, Leah! A thank you to Giulia Calligola for designing the cover and being a fantastic person overall. I'm sure I asked you a million questions, but the cover is perfect. A thank you to my past and present readers for your continued aid and contributions to my characters and their world. I couldn't keep writing books and short story collections without you. Last, I want to give another shout-out to those who crowdfunded the book. I listed all your names on the previous page, but I'm so grateful for the funds you donated to make this project a reality. Thank you, thank you, thank you! I can't wait to share my next project with you. I think you're going to love it!

XOXO

J.S. Living

Also by J.S. Living

The Covenant of Blood

The Brotherhood of Blood (Coming Soon)

* 9 7 9 8 9 8 5 7 0 0 1 3 8 *